This story is adapted from *Hikayat Sha'biyya min Al-Khalij*
published in 1994 by the Centre of Folk Literature, Doha, Qatar

This book would not have been possible without the generous support of

Published in 2006 by JERBOA BOOKS
PO BOX 333838 Dubai UAE
www.jerboabooks.com
ISBN 9948-431-08-1

The King
and
his Three Daughters

Denys Johnson-Davies

Illustrations Sabine P Moser

Once upon a time there was a King
who had three daughters.

When the King's wife died, he built small
palaces for each of his young daughters
and then he visited them regularly every morning.

One day, he had the idea of testing his daughters'
love for him.

He went on his usual visit to his eldest daughter and
enquired of her:
'O Daughter of mine, how much do you love me?'

His eldest daughter answered him:
'I love you, Father of mine, just as I love honey.'

The King left his daughter's palace, happy
and certain about her love for him.

He then paid a visit to his middle daughter and asked
her the same question.

'I love you, Father of mine, in the same way I love sugar,'
she answered.

Once again the father was happy with his daughter's answer.

When he visited the youngest of his daughters and
asked her how much she loved him, he was
surprised at her answer.

'I love you, O Father, in the same way as I love salt,'
she answered.
This answer didn't at all please the King.

'Like salt, did you say?' he asked angrily.
'Yes, Father,' she answered.

A dark frown came over the King's face as he turned away from his
daughter with the words:

'Collect up your clothes and leave this castle. This is no longer
your home and I do not want to see your face again.'

The girl wrapped up a few of her clothes into a bundle
and went out into the darkness of the night,
not knowing where to go.

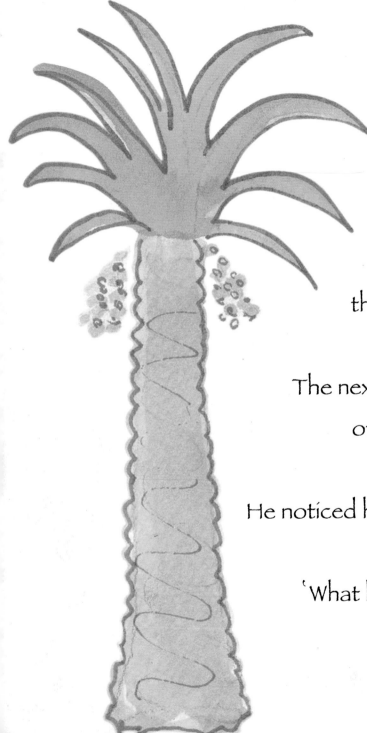

After walking for several days
she arrived at the palace
of a neighbouring King.

She curled herself up under a tree at
the entrance to the palace and fell asleep.

The next morning one of the princes came out
of the palace and saw the girl.

He noticed her ragged clothes and took pity on her.

'What has brought you here, young lady?'
he asked her.

'I came here in search of work,' the girl answered.

The Prince took her into his father's palace and asked
the woman in charge to find some work for her.

Several days later the Prince went into the kitchens
of the palace and found the young girl there.

She had been put in charge of the many
people working in the kitchens.

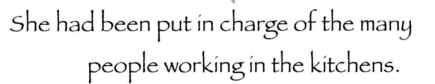
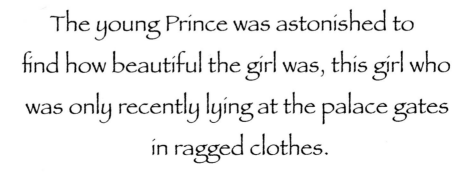

The young Prince was astonished to
find how beautiful the girl was, this girl who
was only recently lying at the palace gates
in ragged clothes.

So struck was the Prince by her fine features and noble bearing that he decided he would like to have her as a wife.

When he told his father of his wish to marry this girl, the King was naturally offended by the thought that his son wished to marry someone who was working in the palace kitchens.

'Are you serious in asking me for my permission that you may marry a maidservant?' he asked.

'Yes, Father,' answered the son.

'She may be a maidservant but she has the looks and manners of someone of high birth. All of that is unimportant. What is important is that I wish to make this young girl my wife. Love, I believe, knows no boundaries.'

Seeing that his son was so determined to have her as his wife, the King finally agreed to the marriage, and soon the news spread among the people that the king's son had married a lowly maidservant.

Several years passed, with the two living together in great happiness. Then the King fell ill and died and the throne passed to his son, and so his wife became the Queen.

One day, news reached them that the King of the neighbouring country was to pay them a visit.

The Queen was not happy about the visit.
Was not this King from the neighbouring country none other than her own father who had thrown her out into the street?

However, she decided not to tell her husband about who the visiting King was.

Great preparations were made for the royal visit, particularly in the kitchens where all the choicest foods were specially cooked.

The Queen herself supervised all the different activities in the kitchens and was insistent about one thing:

'There is to be no salt in any of the food,' she ordered.
The cooks were astonished but did not dare disobey an order given by the Queen.

And so the great day came when the neighbouring King was entertained in the palace.

There was a fine display of different foods that had been cooked for the royal guest.

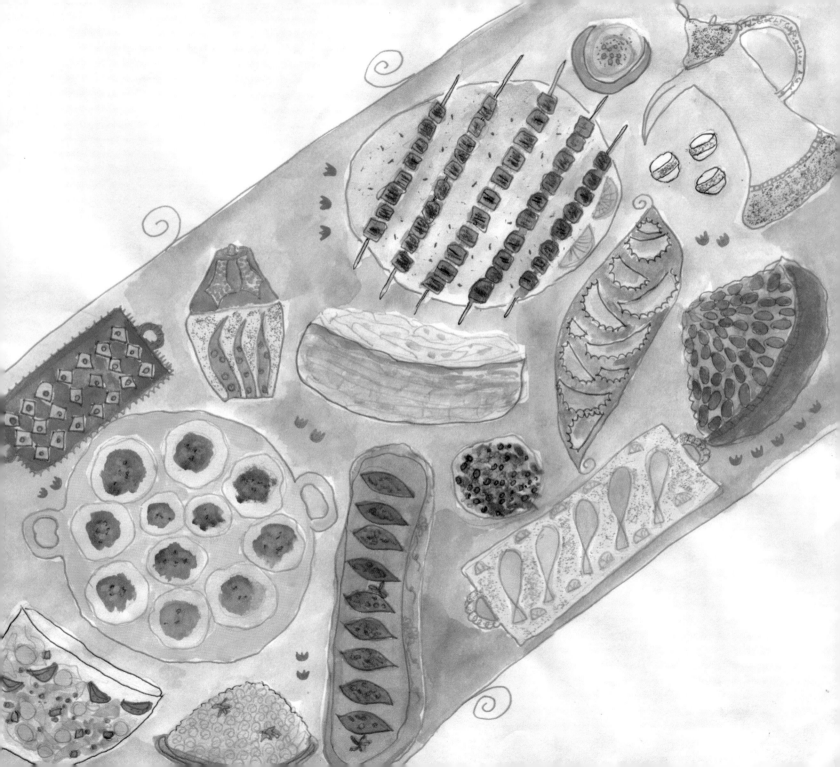

As he tried each dish, his hand would quickly move on to another for he found that all the different foods had been cooked without any salt and therefore had no real taste.

'It seems that Your Majesty does not find our food to be to his liking,' the Queen said to him.

The guest did not know what to reply, for it was true that he could not find a single dish that he really enjoyed.

The Queen explained: 'Perhaps that is because the food has all been cooked without salt. We had heard that Your Majesty did not like salt,' she continued, 'and that once, years ago, you had driven your own daughter from your palace beacuse she had said that her love for you was like her love for salt.'

The King was taken aback by these words. Only then did he look closely at her face and see that this was his own daughter, whose love for him was as her love for something that no one can do without.

Taking his daughter into his arms, he asked forgiveness from her,
for what he had done all those years ago.
The Queen still loved her father and was happy to forgive him, so once again
father and daughter were together as fathers and daughters should be.

Denys Johnson-Davies has been called 'the pioneer translator of modern Arabic literature'.

He has also made a name for himself as a writer of children's books, of which he has published more than thirty titles.

He lives in Marrakesh, Morocco.

Photograph by Paola Crociani

Sabine P Moser is married, mother of three and a kindergarten teacher.

She recently moved back to Austria, having lived in Dubai from 1999 to 2004.

During her stay she began to write and illustrate stories about an aptly named camel, Camel-O-Shy.

Tales of Arabia

More Tales for you to enjoy!

A Tale from the Emirates

Deenoh and Arbab

This is the story of two little goats and their encounter with a wicked witch.
We follow their mother as she challenges the witch and good wins over evil.

A Tale from Qatar

The Woodcutter

Struggling to feed his family, the woodcutter discovers a genie in a tree in the
forest. The genie takes pity on the poor woodcutter, but his foolishness leads
him into trouble over and over again. Will he ever learn?

A Tale from Oman

The Great Warrior Ali

Ali's father was a great warrior and Ali wants to be just like him. He's never had
any training as a warrior but somehow manages to convince everyone he is a
great swordsman. We follow his adventures in this wonderful tale from Oman.